RAIDERS of the LOST ARK™
The Storybook Based on the Movie

Random House   New York

Based on the film *Raiders of the Lost Ark*
Screenplay by Lawrence Kasdan
Story by George Lucas and Philip Kaufman

Editor, Lucasfilm, Ltd.: Ann Holler

Storybook adaptation by Les Martin

Library of Congress Cataloging in Publication Data: Martin, Les, [date]. Raiders of the lost ark: the storybook based on the movie. SUMMARY: An American archaeology professor becomes involved in an attempt to prevent the Nazis from locating a sacred Hebrew relic which, according to legend, has awesome, supernatural power. [1. Adventure stories] I. Lucas, George. II. Raiders of the lost ark. [Motion picture] III. Title. PZ7.M36353Rai [Fic] 80-27330 ISBN: 0-394-84802-0 (trade); ISBN: 0-394-94802-5 (lib. bdg.)
Manufactured in the United States of America   3 4 5 6 7 8 9 0

TM   Trademark owned by Lucasfilm, Ltd.

The Lost Ark
The coveted golden chest that once carried the Ten Commandments

Marion Ravenwood
The beautiful daughter of a famous archaeologist

Indiana "Indy" Jones
A dedicated archaeologist — and a daring adventurer

René Belloq
A ruthless Frenchman who is Indy's greatest rival

Sallah
The most skillful archaeological worker in Egypt

Toht
A Nazi henchman

Imam
A wise Egyptian astrologer

Katanga
The captain of the ship *Bantu Wind*

Dietrich
The officer in charge of the Nazi search for the Lost Ark

The year was 1936. In Germany, Adolf Hitler had risen to supreme power as head of the Nazi Party, and was arming his country for war.

In Washington, D.C., the leaders of the United States watched uneasily as the shadow of Nazi imperialism fell over Europe.

But even as the threat of global war grew every day, most Americans were thinking of their own personal difficulties, their own hopes and dreams.

This was certainly true of Indiana Jones. Indy stood in a clearing deep in a South American jungle. His handsome face was streaked with grime and sweat under his battered felt hat. His chin was covered with stubble. For days he and his two Peruvian guides had been struggling through the uncharted green maze of the tropical rain forest. But now, as he looked across the clearing he had come to, Indy forgot how tired he had been. He felt fresh and strong and eager.

At last, Indy had found the entrance to the ancient temple he had been searching for. Long ago, Chachapoyan Indians had built this temple to protect a small golden statue they worshiped as a god. Somewhere inside the temple was the statue.

Indiana Jones wanted that statue. He wanted it very badly. Nothing was going to stop him from getting it. Not all the cunning defenses of the ancient temple builders. And not the modern pistol that was pointing at him right now.

Barranca, one of Indy's guides, held the pistol. Barranca had decided that he wanted the golden statue for himself.

Indy's hand moved to the back of his leather jacket faster than Barranca could blink. Out from under the jacket came a tightly curled bullwhip. The ten-foot leather lash of the whip whistled through the air. It wrapped around Barranca's gun hand, jerking the guide's hand down. The gun went off, and the bullet buried itself in the ground. With a gasp of pain, Barranca let the pistol drop.

"You'd better leave it there," advised Indy. "I'd rather not have to show you what else this whip can do."

Barranca looked at the whip resting lightly in Indy's hand. Without a word, he turned and fled into the jungle.

"That Barranca was crazy," said Satipo, the second guide. "But you can trust me, *Señor*. I am your loyal servant. You can put away your whip."

"We'll see how loyal you are," said Indy. "Follow me. We're going into the temple."

"But the curse," Satipo protested fearfully. "It is my duty as your guide to warn you of the Curse of the Ancients."

"Come *on*, Satipo," Indy said. "A little thing like the threat of death shouldn't discourage you. It's all part of the job."

Indy led the way inside. Holding lighted torches, the two men scrambled down a stone incline and along a twisting tunnel. Tarantulas scurried underfoot. The air was heavy with the smell of centuries. Then, around a turn in the tunnel, the two men saw the end of the passageway, ablaze with light.

The sight made Satipo forget his fear. He pressed forward past Indy—and screamed.

The guide had stepped into empty space. He was falling into a bottomless hole concealed by a layer of cobwebs. Just in time, Indy grabbed Satipo's belt and pulled him back.

"We must stop now," said Satipo, shaking with fear. "There is no way we can go around this hole."

Indy looked upward. "But we can go *over* it," he said.

Satipo was puzzled. "How, *Señor*?"

"With this." Indy drew out his whip and lashed the end of it around a root hanging from the ceiling. "Do you want to be first across, Satipo?"

The terrified look on Satipo's face was answer enough. Indy took hold of the whip handle and swung himself easily across the yawning black pit. Then he swung the whip back to Satipo. Satipo's mouth moved in a silent prayer. Holding on to the whip for dear life, the guide landed next to Indy with a thud.

"Nothing like a little fun to liven up a trip," said Indy. "Now let's see about getting the idol."

A moment later they were at the end of the passageway, staring into a small stone chamber. Its floor was made of tile, laid in an intricate design. Its walls were decorated with a strange pattern of thousands of tiny holes. In the middle of the room, sitting on a stone altar, was the golden idol. Indy's breath stopped when he saw it. Lit by a single shaft of bright sunlight, the gleaming statue looked both beautiful and eerie.

"So, there is nothing to fear after all," said Satipo. "We have not been hurt. Let me get the idol for you." He started into the chamber.

"No!" Indy blocked Satipo's way. Without another word, he

picked up a stick and tapped one of the border tiles. Nothing happened. Then he tapped a center tile. Suddenly there was a rush of air and a whistling sound. A swarm of deadly darts flew from the tiny holes in the wall. They were aimed to kill any intruder.

"I thought our ancient friends would try to defend their god," said Indy. "I'm glad they didn't disappoint me."

Careful to step only on the border tiles, Indy made his way across the room to where the idol rested. He stood enjoying his first good look at it. To some people, the gold statue might have looked ugly, even frightening. To Indy, it was a feast of beauty. Looking at it made him feel as if he had stepped back through time. He reached out to grasp the statue and then remembered where he was.

Indy drew his hand back. He could sense the genius of the temple builders all around him. What other cunning traps had they laid to protect their precious idol? He was sure he hadn't outwitted them yet.

Indy emptied out his leather coin pouch. Then he filled it with dirt from around the altar base. He weighed the pouch in his palm. It might — just might — now weigh the same as the idol. If he put the pouch in the idol's place at the exact moment that he lifted the idol from the altar, chances were he might — just might — get away with the switch.

"There's only one way to find out," Indy said to himself. He made the switch. For a moment, nothing happened. Then a stone slab on the altar fell with a sharp click. Indy heard a deep rumbling from behind the chamber walls. It grew louder, and the entire temple started to shake.

Clutching the idol, Indy raced back on the border tiles to the doorway. Satipo had already started down the passageway ahead of him, and was using the whip to swing across the pit.

When he was safely on the other side, Satipo shouted, "Throw me the idol. Then I will give you back your whip."

A falling stone from the ceiling hit Indy's cheek. He had no time to argue. He tossed the idol to Satipo. Satipo caught the idol and stuffed it into his jacket. Then he dropped the whip on the ground.

"Adios, amigo," he shouted to Indy, and disappeared around the curve in the tunnel.

Indy didn't bother to answer. With every ounce of his strength, he hurled himself across the pit. He fell short, and began a sickening drop down. Then his clawing fingers caught the side of the pit. Painfully, he pulled himself up.

Above the rumbling of the collapsing temple came an anguished scream. It was Satipo. When Indy reached him, the thief was dead. Long spikes had sprung out of the wall and into his fleeing body. The curse had claimed its victim.

"Adios, amigo," said Indy as he took the idol from Satipo's jacket. He had no time to lose. The walls of the passageway were crumbling. The stone floor was splitting apart. With his lungs bursting, Indy made it out of the temple seconds before it caved in.

Panting, he threw himself on the ground. He looked at the idol glowing in the sunshine. He grinned. Nearby, on a jungle river, a seaplane waited to fly him back to civilization. Soon the idol would rest in a museum, where the world could enjoy its beauty. At a moment like this, Indy knew why he loved taking risks. Beating all the odds made triumph taste delicious.

Suddenly, Indy's grin faded. On the ground he saw a shadow lengthening toward the idol. He looked up to meet the amused glance of his greatest rival — the Frenchman René Belloq.

Belloq, like Indy, was an archaeologist who loved to hunt the lost treasures of the past. Like Indy he possessed great knowledge and great determination. But there the resemblances ended. Indy's discoveries went to universities and museums, where they could be studied and enjoyed. Belloq's were hoarded for his solitary pleasure — or sold to private collectors for huge sums of money. The Frenchman was dishonest, clever, and ruthless. Indy despised him.

Even deep in the jungle, Belloq looked elegant. His safari suit was spotless. His pith helmet was white. His boots were as brightly polished as his smile.

"We meet again," said Belloq. "As always, it is a pleasure to see you, Indy Jones. You've gone to such trouble to get me something I want. Now, please, give me the idol. Unless you prefer to argue with my friends."

Belloq was flanked by two giant Hovitos warriors. Their glistening bodies were bright with war paint, their blowguns ready to spit out poison darts. At the jungle's edge were thirty more warriors.

"When you put it so politely, how can I say no?" said Indy with a wry grimace. He got to his feet, holding out the idol to Belloq. Belloq grabbed it eagerly, and made the mistake Indy had been hoping for.

Belloq held the idol high above his head for the Hovitos warriors to admire. Instantly they fell to their knees before the god of their ancestors. Belloq just can't resist playing god, Indy thought. Then he made his break into the jungle.

In a flash, Belloq and the Hovitos were after him. Indy could hear them gaining on him as he fought his way through the thick foliage. He barely made it to the edge of a high cliff. Far below was the river, where his seaplane waited. There was just one way to reach it. Indy dove. He swam to the plane and dragged himself aboard, drenched and gasping for breath. "Get it going," he said to the pilot, "or we're both dead men."

As the plane lifted into the sky, Indy looked down at the jungle. But all he could see in his mind was the idol in Belloq's hand. "Enjoy it while you can, Belloq," Indy muttered. "When I catch up with you, I'm going to make you pay for it and everything else you've stolen—with interest."

At the American college where he taught, Indy Jones was a classroom hero. His students knew him as a dedicated scholar, whose love and knowledge of ancient civilizations made him an inspiring teacher. Marcus Brody, curator of the University Museum, knew Indy's other side.

The two of them were in Indy's office now. Indy was pleading, "Give me just two thousand dollars. I'll track down Belloq wherever he is. I'll bring the idol back for your museum."

"Listen to me, Indy," said Brody. "You'll have to forget about Belloq for the moment. There are some men waiting outside to see you. Important men."

Brody opened the door and two men came in. "Let me introduce Colonel Musgrove and Major Eaton of U.S. Army Intelligence," said Brody.

"Pleased to meet you, gentlemen," said Indy. "But tell me, what can a humble archaeologist do for you?"

"Do you know Professor Abner Ravenwood?" asked Colonel Musgrove.

"I studied under him," said Indy. He had stopped smiling.

"Where is he now?" asked Major Eaton.

"I don't know," said Indy. "We had . . . an argument. I haven't seen him for years."

"Too bad," said the Colonel. "I was hoping you could help us."

"I'd like to, if it has anything to do with helping him. I owe him a lot," said Indy. "He's not in trouble, is he?"

"We're not sure," said Major Eaton. "Let me fill you in. As you must know, Hitler and his Nazi followers have been arming Germany for war. From all reports, their long-range goal is world domination. What you may not know is that Hitler is a firm believer in the power of the occult. His agents have been searching all over the globe for ancient relics—relics that will give him 'supernatural power.' Hitler wants to be more than just a leader. He wants to be a god."

"I know a certain Frenchman he should meet. They could fight it out for first place," said Indy,

half to himself. Then to the Major and the Colonel he said, "But what does this have to do with Professor Ravenwood?"

"Right now there is a huge Nazi expedition hunting relics in Egypt," said Colonel Musgrove. "Last week we intercepted one of their messages back to Germany." The Colonel pulled out a piece of paper and read, *"We have found Tanis. Now we must acquire the headpiece of the Staff of Ra from Professor Ravenwood of the United States."*

"My God," said Indy, his voice excited. "They've found Tanis."

"And just what is Tanis?" asked the Major.

Indy's eyes lit with enthusiasm. "The City of Tanis may well be the hiding place of the Lost Ark."

"The Lost Ark?" asked the Colonel, bewildered.

"The Ark of the Covenant. The chest that the Israelites used to carry the Ten Commandments."

"You don't mean *the* Ten Commandments?" asked the Major.

Indy replied as if he were talking to a slow student. "I mean the stone tablets the commandments were written on. The ones Moses brought down from the mountain. He smashed the tablets in anger when he saw his people breaking the commandments. But the pieces were saved and put in the Ark. The Israelites carried the Ark with them wherever they went."

"Amazing," said the Colonel.

"Hard to believe," said the Major.

"Let me show you something," said Indy. He pulled a scroll from his bookshelf and unrolled it carefully. "Look at this picture." The men gathered around to examine it closely.

The army of Israel was facing its fleeing enemies. In the front ranks of the Israelites, two soldiers carried a beautiful chest suspended from long poles. The chest was crowned by a pair of sculptured angels. From the wings of the angels came a bright, piercing light. This light burned into the enemy army, destroying it in flames.

"If what this picture shows is true," said Indy, "that's what the Lost Ark looks like. And that's what it can do."

"My God, what a weapon!" said the Colonel.

"According to the Bible," said Indy, "the army that carries the Ark cannot be defeated."

"*If* you believe in that sort of thing," said the Major.

"Hitler believes in it," said the Colonel. He turned to Indy. "Professor Jones, you said the Lost Ark is in Tanis. That means the Nazis must have their hands on it by now."

"Not quite," said Indy. "They can't find the Lost Ark without the Staff of Ra. Let me show you another picture."

Indy went to the blackboard and drew a long stick. On top of this he drew a circle with an eye at its center. "The Staff of Ra consisted of two parts," he said. "A staff, about five or six feet long, and a headpiece, made of metal. At the center of the headpiece was a crystal eye."

"Very interesting," said the Major. "But what did this Staff of Ra do?"

"It was the key to finding the hiding place of the Lost Ark," said Indy. "You see, the Ark was stolen from the Israelites in 980 B.C., by an Egyptian pharaoh. He hid it in Tanis. Then the city was buried by a sandstorm that lasted a whole year." Indy smiled. "That storm has been called the wrath of God."

"But what about the staff, and the headpiece?" asked the Major impatiently.

"According to old manuscripts," Indy said, "there was a room in Tanis called the Map Room. This room held an exact model of the city, in miniature.

"When the Staff of Ra was placed in the right spot in the Map Room, at a certain time of day, something remarkable would happen. Sunlight coming into the room would pass through the crystal eye of the headpiece and hit the model of Tanis. The spot where the sunbeam hit showed the location of a secret chamber called the Well of the Souls. And the Well of the Souls, gentlemen, may just be the hiding place of the Lost Ark of the Covenant."

"What a wild story," said the Major. He mopped his brow, as if the office had suddenly become too hot for him.

"You say that Abner Ravenwood has the headpiece?" the Colonel asked.

"He found it years ago," said Indy. "But he never got to use it, because he couldn't find Tanis."

"And you say you don't know where Ravenwood is now?" the Colonel continued.

"The last I heard of him, he was going off to hunt relics in Asia," said Indy.

"Well, that's that," said the Major, putting on his hat.

The Colonel didn't move. The look he gave the Major told him not to move either.

"We're in an awkward position," the Colonel said to Indy. "Officially, we can't act on the story you've told us. We have no real proof that it's true."

"You can say that again," said the Major, before the Colonel silenced him with another look.

"Of course, if someone could *bring* us proof, that would be different," said the Colonel. "That someone would have to find Ra-

venwood. Persuade him to give up the headpiece. Use the headpiece to find the Lost Ark in Tanis. And bring the Ark back to us." The Colonel looked hard at Indy. "Naturally, it would be an advantage if that person knew Ravenwood well. If he knew about the Lost Ark too, so much the better."

"The Ark," said Indy, his eyes gleaming, "is the greatest mystery of all time. An archaeologist's dream."

Marcus Brody had been listening quietly. Now he asked the Colonel, "Do you think you could pay that someone for the job? Say, five thousand dollars?"

"We could afford that," said the Colonel. "Plus travel expenses."

"But that's *all* the help we could give on such a *peculiar* project," said the Major. "The man we hire would be completely on his own. He'd have to understand something about the Nazis. They don't like interference. And they can get very rough."

"What do you say?" the Colonel asked Indy. "Remember, even as we stand here talking, the Nazis may be moving closer to Professor Ravenwood — and to the Lost Ark."

"You don't seem to realize that I'm a respectable college professor," said Indy. "I can't just drop everything this minute to take off on some crazy adventure. It'll take me a while to get ready." Indy began loosening his tie. "At least an hour."

Swirling snow filled the night air. As Indy trudged through the subzero darkness, he felt as if he had landed on another planet.

But this was still the earth—the very ends of it: Nepal, home of the highest mountains in the world, the terrifying Himalayas. Indy had followed Abner Ravenwood's trail to this desolate place. Squinting through the snow, he made out a faint light. He moved toward it and saw a battered building on the edge of a tiny village. The sign above the door read: "The Raven."

Indy's stomach tightened. There was a good chance he would find his old professor inside. Indy did not know what he could say to him after all the years of silence. The collapse of their friendship had been painful—too painful to think about until now.

Indy pushed the door open. He walked into the harsh light and loud noise of the mountain saloon. It was crowded with rough characters—bearded mountain climbers, beady-eyed smugglers, thieves, and pickpockets. All of them looked drunk.

Suddenly Indy froze as he saw someone he knew. It was not Professor Ravenwood but Marion, his daughter. She was as beautiful now as when Indy had seen her last, ten years ago.

He forced himself to walk up to her. "Hello, Marion," he said. "You haven't changed a bit."

She looked at Indy a moment as if she couldn't believe her eyes. Then she swung her right fist to catch Indy square on the jaw.

"I guess I was wrong," said Indy, rubbing his jaw. "You *have* changed."

"Get out of here right now," Marion said. "I don't want to see you ever again."

"Relax," said Indy. "It's not you I want to see. I'm looking for your father."

"You're a little late," said Marion. "Dad vanished in an avalanche two years ago."

"I'm sorry," said Indy.

"It's too late to be sorry," said Marion. "For that—or for anything else." She started to turn away.

"Marion, wait," said Indy. "I need your help."

"Why should I help you?" she asked bitterly. "You walked out of my life without saying a word— just because Dad found out we were in love."

"Your father was right to make me go," said Indy. "I was wrong to get involved with you. You were much too young."

"Well, I'm all grown up now," said Marion. "I'm a successful businesswoman—if you can call running this three-ring circus of a bar a business. Now tell me, what's *your* business here?"

"I'm looking for a relic that your father had," said Indy. "It's a medallion in the shape of the sun with an amber crystal at its center."

"My father and his relics," said Marion. "He spent his life looking for them. He died looking for them. I don't want to talk about them!"

"Look, you said you were a businesswoman," said Indy. "I'm willing to pay."

"How much?" she asked.

"Three thousand dollars," said Indy.

"Five thousand," said Marion. "I'd like to go back to America in style."

"Okay," said Indy. "Five thousand. Give me the relic and I'll pay you. Then we'll call it quits."

"Not so fast," said Marion. "I didn't say I had it, did I? I just *might* have it. Come back tomorrow, and I'll let you know."

"I'm in a hurry," said Indy. "Why don't we make it later tonight?"

"All right," said Marion. "Later tonight, after I get the customers out of here. Hurry or not, you'll have to wait that long."

"Fine," said Indy. "See you later." He turned to go.

"Wait," said Marion. "Leave the money with me. I want you to learn to trust me—just as I trusted you."

"I guess I have to play it your way," said Indy, handing her the $5,000 in cash that the U.S. Army had given him.

"I guess this time you do," said Marion.

When Indy came back to the Raven after midnight, Marion was not alone.

Four men were with her. Their leader was a short, stocky German named Toht. Spectacles glinted on his fleshy face, and his mouth was a cruel line. In one of Toht's hands was a gun. In the other was a poker with a red-hot tip.

The other men were armed as well. A second German, in a trench coat, carried a submachine gun. A nasty-looking Mongolian had one, too. Beside him, a shifty-eyed Nepalese held a long, wicked knife.

Indy stood in the doorway and watched as Marion backed away from the intruders. Then Indy saw something else. On top of the bar gleamed a round medallion with a crystal eye at its center — the headpiece of the Staff of Ra. Marion must have dropped it there when the men broke in. Fortunately it was partially concealed by whiskey bottles. The intruders hadn't seen it yet.

"Wait," said Marion, as Toht came at her. "I've changed my mind. I'll tell you where it is. Maybe we can make a deal for it."

"This is what I make my deals with," snarled Toht. He aimed the glowing poker tip straight at Marion's face.

"What the . . . !" yelled the Nazi agent as the lash of Indy's bullwhip wrapped around the poker. The poker was jerked out

of Toht's hands. It flew through the air and crashed through the window — but not before it had touched a curtain and set the flimsy cloth on fire.

At first no one noticed the spreading flames. Everyone was too busy fighting. A shot from Indy's pistol disposed of the Nepalese. Marion grabbed an ax handle and knocked out the Mongolian. By this time Toht and the other German were crouched behind overturned tables, waiting for their

chance to get a clear shot at Indy.

Marion dropped her ax handle and picked up the fallen Mongolian's submachine gun. She was trying to figure out how to work it when she heard a crash. A giant Sherpa had smashed through the door. He jumped Indy from behind. The two of them rolled on the floor in hand-to-hand combat.

Toht saw his chance. He rose to his feet and aimed his pistol at Indy.

Suddenly there was an explosion. The flames had reached the whiskey bottles and turned them into firebombs. The fire blazed everywhere. It was then that Toht saw the headpiece lying on the bar. He grabbed it and screamed out in agony, as the smell of burning flesh filled the air. The searing-hot metal headpiece had burned its design into the skin of his hand. Toht dropped the headpiece and ran out into the night, to plunge his aching hand into the snow.

By now the second German was on his feet. He aimed his submachine gun at Indy, who was still struggling with the Sherpa. The German's finger tightened on the trigger. Then he was blasted off his feet. Marion had figured out how her gun worked.

A moment later, Indy stood up. The giant Sherpa lay motionless on the floor. As Indy picked up his battered felt hat and put it back on his head, a burning beam from the ceiling came crashing down in front of him.

"Let's get out of here!" he said.

"Don't you want your precious Egyptian relic?" she asked.

"I want to get out of this death-trap alive," said Indy.

"You should have the head-piece," Marion said. She picked up the hot metal with a thick piece of cloth torn from her shirt. "After all, you paid for it." Then she said, "My God, I forgot the money!" She looked down the bar. All that was left of the $5,000 was a small pile of ashes.

"Worry about that later," said Indy, pulling her toward the door.

The two of them stood side by

side in the freezing night. Before long the flames had eaten up the last of the Raven.

"Thanks for the headpiece," said Indy, "and for saving my life. I owe you a lot."

"You sure do," said Marion. "You owe me for the bar you just burned down. And you owe me the five thousand dollars that just burned up."

"You're really something," said Indy, grinning at her.

"I *am* something," said Marion. "As long as I have this headpiece, I'm your partner!"

Under the brutal sun, the narrow, crowded street in Cairo, Egypt, was almost as hot as the burning Raven. Clouds of dust rose in the air. Veiled women walked two by two. Peddlers shouted their offerings to passersby. Ragged beggars pleaded for coins. City dwellers in suits and desert Arabs in flowing robes jostled one another. Now and then an overloaded bus or a horn-blowing auto wove through the steady stream of people.

Indy Jones made his way along the street as fast as he could, with Marion beside him. He barely noticed the crowd. His mind was on the vast, empty desert that began just a few miles outside of the city. He wished he could see what the Nazis were doing there. Had they succeeded in bringing the ancient city of Tanis to light?

"Where are we going?" Marion asked him as she dodged the hand of a beggar.

"We're going to see an Egyptian named Sallah," Indy said. "He's an old friend of mine. He's also the best digger in Cairo. If the Germans are really serious about uncovering Tanis, they're sure to be using him."

At Sallah's house, Indy soon found out he was right.

"I was there yesterday, when they found the Map Room of Tanis," Sallah told him as they sipped thick, black coffee in his shadowed courtyard. A small monkey with an intelligent, almost human, face sat at Marion's feet. Its bright little eyes moved with lively curiosity from Sallah to Indy to Marion, as if it were following their conversation. "The room was in perfect condition," Sallah went on, shaking his head in wonder. "The model city is there, intact."

"So the story of Tanis is turning out to be true," said Indy.

"I'm afraid it is," said Sallah. His normally cheerful face looked worried. "I'm *very* afraid it is. I do not want to think what can happen if the Lost Ark is really there in Tanis, waiting to be discovered. It is not something people today are meant to possess."

Indy was worried, too—but for a different reason.

"The Nazis are moving much faster than I thought they could," he said.

"They have an expert helping them," said Sallah.

"You mean yourself?" said Indy.

"Of course not," said Sallah. "You know what I think of the Nazis. I dig slowly for them—as slowly as I can. But they have a man who knows more about ancient Egypt than anyone I have ever met, except you, Indy Jones. He is a real expert. I am not surprised that the Nazis take orders from him, even though he is a Frenchman."

Indy could just manage to say the word. *"Belloq."*

"Belloq," said Sallah. "Yes, that is his name. Belloq. This is bad news for you, I see."

"It's bad news and good news at the same time," said Indy. "It means that I've got a real fight on my hands." He grinned. "That's the good news. The bad news is that Belloq is too close to the Ark for comfort. Thank God he doesn't have the headpiece. He'd need incredible luck to find the Well of the Souls and the Lost Ark without it."

"You know, Indy, even though you are my good friend, I wish you did not have the headpiece," said Sallah. "Forgive me for saying so, but it is not meant for *anyone* to find the Lost Ark."

"But I do have the headpiece," said Indy. "And I'm going to use it. And I ask you as a friend to help me."

"As a friend, I cannot refuse," said Sallah.

Indy placed the headpiece on the table. Sallah leaned forward to inspect it.

At that same moment, the monkey at Marion's feet leaped onto the table. As it put its face close to the headpiece, its bright eyes gleamed.

"What a cute pet you have, Sallah," said Marion, stroking the monkey.

"This creature does not belong to my household," said Sallah. "I thought it came in with you."

"Maybe it did," said Marion. "See how it likes me." At that moment, as if understanding her words, the monkey planted a kiss on her nose. "I think I'll adopt it," said Marion. "It can look after *my* share of the headpiece."

"You make an absolutely perfect couple," said Indy. Then his face became serious again. "Sallah, can you make anything of the markings on the metal? I've never seen anything like them."

"No," said Sallah. "But I know somebody who might. I will give you his address."

"I'll go see him right away," said Indy.

"May Allah go with you," said Sallah.

"Thanks," said Indy. "I'll need all the help I can get."

Out on the street again, Indy hurried along. Marion almost had to break into a run to keep up with him. Suddenly she cried, "Indy, wait a minute!"

"What is it?" he asked, turning back to her.

"My monkey," she said. "He jumped off my shoulder and ran away."

Indy stared at Marion in disbelief. "Here we are, in a desperate race against time. We're on the verge of solving one of the greatest riddles of the ages. And you're worried about a monkey!"

"You're just like my father was," said Marion. "As soon as you start hunting one of your precious relics, you forget about everything else."

"Don't worry about the monkey," said Indy. "It will find you again. It knows the city a lot better than we do."

Indy was right. The monkey knew the city very well indeed. It raced through the maze of streets and squares. Within minutes it

had found its master. It snapped to attention and gave him a sharp Nazi salute.

"You are so clever, my little one," its trainer said. "You are the very best agent I have. Now lead me and my men to the Americans!"

Indy and Marion had just entered a tiny square crowded with peddlers' stands when Indy stiffened. He threw his arm in front of Marion to stop her from going any farther. A cutthroat crew was closing in on them from all sides. It was a murderous mix of Nazis and Arabs, armed with guns, swords, and daggers.

In a flash, Indy's bullwhip was in his hand. Marion grabbed a thick broom handle from a nearby stand. The peddler loudly demanded to be paid for it, but ducked for cover when the action started.

Indy flicked out his bullwhip and jerked it tightly around an Arab's chest. Marion whacked a German skull with her broom handle and held her weapon ready to strike again. But an Arab sliced his sword through it as if the wood were butter. Marion was left holding a useless stump.

Indy used his bullwhip handle to knock the Arab out. He grabbed Marion's arm and half-threw her into an alleyway. "Run for your life!" he ordered.

"Not without you!" she answered.

"Stubborn as always," said Indy, and slammed a high wooden gate shut between them. Marion started beating at the gate. "Save your strength for running!" he yelled at her. Then he turned to face the advancing Germans and Arabs, his bullwhip in one hand, his .45 pistol in the other.

Marion gave one more futile smash of her fist against the gate.

Then she started running. Perhaps she could find help for Indy.

What she found was a huge Arab blocking her path. His eyes lit up when he saw her. A dagger flashed in his hand. Marion ducked into an open doorway. She found herself in a small courtyard with no other way out. The Arab eagerly followed her in. Marion picked up a heavy clay pot, and smashed it down on the Arab's head. He fell, unconscious.

There were running footsteps in the alleyway outside, and a voice shouting orders in German. Marion saw a large wicker basket in the courtyard corner. She climbed into it, pulling the cover over her head. She had found the perfect hiding place.

On top of the courtyard wall, the monkey watched Marion's move with great interest. When Marion's head vanished under the basket cover, the monkey clapped its hands together as if applauding. Then it ran off happily to find its master.

Meanwhile, Indy had opened the gate and entered the alleyway. Behind him the square was littered with battered bodies and smashed stalls. The peddlers were coming out of hiding and rearranging their wares.

Indy moved cautiously down the alley, on the lookout for an ambush. He inched around a curve. Far down the alley he saw two Arabs carrying a large wicker basket. With them was a trench-coated German. Then Indy heard Marion's voice, from inside the basket. She was screaming for help. In the next moment, they all disappeared. There was only a patch of light at the end of the alley—and dead silence.

Indy dashed to the end of the alley and stood there with his heart pounding. He couldn't see the Arabs, the Nazi, or the wicker basket. All he could see was a huge square filled with beggars—the most deformed cripples in all of Cairo. Moving through this strange mob was a coffin held high by wailing mourners and chanting priests.

Through a break in the crowd, Indy spotted a truck loaded with wicker baskets on the far side of the square. The German in the trench coat was at the wheel.

Indy fought his way past the pleading hands of the beggars. He ignored the angry shouts of mourners as he cut through their procession. He heard the truck engine roar into motion and saw its tires begin to turn. There was just one way to stop it. Indy took aim with his .45. He pulled the trigger. Then everything went out of control.

The bullet hit the front tire of the truck. At the same moment, the Nazi at the wheel pressed the accelerator. The truck jumped into high speed — and smashed into a wall. It burst into flames and a gigantic explosion ripped the air. The shock waves hit Indy full in the face, half-stunning him. All around him beggars were scurrying, hopping, and crawling to safety. The coffin had been dropped and the cloth-wrapped corpse lay forgotten by fleeing mourners. But Indy saw none of this. He stepped, as if sleepwalking, to where the truck had been. All that was left of it was a smoking metal shell. "Marion," he whispered. Then he looked at the gun in his hand, and threw it to the ground.

"It was not your fault," Sallah said to Indy. "You could not have known that the other wicker baskets on the truck were filled with Nazi explosives and ammunition. They killed Marion, not you."

It was night, and the two friends were again sitting in Sallah's courtyard. Sallah had never seen Indy like this. Since Marion Ravenwood had vanished in the explosion that morning, the life had gone out of Indy's eyes.

"If I hadn't brought her here, it never would have happened," Indy said, staring at the ground.

"So you really cared about her," Sallah said.

"What difference does it make now?"

"If you really cared about her," Sallah said, "you would keep working to find the Lost Ark. You would not sit here doing nothing when that Frenchman, Belloq, is about to lead the Nazis to it."

"Belloq?" Indy lifted his head. "Belloq knows where the Lost Ark is?" Indy's eyes began to gleam. "But how can he find it without the headpiece? Don't just sit there, Sallah. Tell me! I have to know."

"I've been trying to tell you," said Sallah. "But you wouldn't listen."

"I'm listening now," Indy said, leaning forward. "What has Belloq come up with?"

"He's come up with the headpiece," said Sallah.

"But *I* have it," said Indy. Quickly his hand went to his pocket. When he felt the headpiece, he sighed with relief. Then his face darkened. "Don't tell me this is a fake."

"No," said Sallah. "But Belloq has an exact copy of it. The only difference is that his has markings on only one side."

"He must have found a picture of the headpiece somewhere," said Indy. His mind began to move into high gear. "The picture would just show one side. He could have had a metal copy made from that." Indy grimaced. "Belloq must be wild with joy."

"He is," said Sallah. "I was there this afternoon when he displayed it. The Nazi commander, Dietrich, was just as happy. They were laughing like fools when they went into the Map Room with it."

"Dietrich is going to have to wait his turn for the Lost Ark," said Indy, thinking out loud. "The Nazis may want it a lot. But if I know Belloq, he wants it, too. And what Belloq wants, he usually takes. Tell me, how close is he to finding it?"

"They gave us orders to dig in a new spot tomorrow," said Sallah. "They put every man they have to work."

"Then we don't have much time," said Indy. He picked up the headpiece and turned it over. "Sallah, remember the man you told me about? The man who can translate these markings? I've got to see him right away."

"I have already thought of that," smiled Sallah. "He is expecting us in an hour."

"Good," said Indy. "Let's—" Then he glanced up in surprise. "Well, look who's here!"

It was the monkey. Leaping down from the top of the courtyard wall, it rubbed against Indy's leg, chattering nervously.

"Let me give you something to nibble on," said Indy. He reached for a plateful of dates that a servant had brought in earlier. "I know Marion would want you to have this."

He tossed the monkey a date. The monkey caught it and swallowed it eagerly. It raised its paws to beg for more. Suddenly it stiffened. Its face froze in agony. It fell dead.

Sallah hastily dropped the date he was about to eat. "The dates are poisoned! The Nazis must know you are here! But how?"

"We'll probably never know," said Indy. "We can just thank our friend here for saving our lives. Too bad he had to lose his own to do it."

"The will of Allah works in mysterious ways," said Sallah, gazing down at the monkey.

Not long after, the two friends stood at the doorway of a small secluded house on the edge of Cairo. An old man dressed in worn robes answered their knock. His eyes were bright in his wrinkled face as he greeted them.

"This is Imam," said Sallah to Indy. "He is one of the few who can read the markings on the headpiece."

"I am happy to meet you," said Indy. He followed Imam into the house and sat down at the old man's work table. "Can you tell us what this means?" he asked, handing him the sun-shaped piece of metal.

The old man peered closely at the markings on one side of the headpiece. "This is a warning. A very strong warning. 'Do not disturb the Ark of the Covenant. Do not touch it. Do not open it. God Himself will show no pity to the one who gazes into it.'"

"That warning won't stop Belloq," said Indy. "It won't stop the Nazis either." He turned to Imam. "Please, go on. What else do the markings say?"

"'Measure a staff six cadem high to show the way to the place no man should go,'" said the old man.

"*Cadem* are the old way of measuring," said Sallah. "Six *cadem* are about seventy-two inches."

"Then Belloq has all he needs to know to find the Ark," said Indy. His shoulders slumped. "Thanks," he said to Imam. "I guess that wraps it all up."

"Please—wait," said Imam. "You young people are too impatient. You must wait to hear what is written on the other side of the headpiece. 'Take one cadem back to honor the Hebrew God whose Ark this is.'"

"Sallah, you said that Belloq's copy of the headpiece had markings on just one side. Are you sure?" asked Indy.

"I saw it with my own eyes," said Sallah.

"Then the staff that Belloq made for the headpiece must be one *cadem* too long! He'll be looking for the Ark in the wrong place!" Indy's face broke into a grin. He jumped up from the table and began to pace as he talked. "We just have to mount *our* headpiece on the right-sized staff. We'll get into the Map Room and take our own reading of where the Well of the Souls is buried. We can beat Belloq to the Ark yet!"

The next morning, Indy stood alone in the Map Room of Tanis. He wore the dirty, ragged clothing of an Egyptian digger. In his hand was a long wooden staff, crowned by the headpiece. Before his eyes was the most amazing sight he had ever seen. It was a model of Tanis, the city in miniature — exactly as it had looked three thousand years ago. Indy bent to look at the buildings, the streets, the squares. For one magic moment he could imagine the people, the horses, the chariots, all the pulsing life of the long-buried city.

Indy tore his gaze away. He had no more time to enjoy this archaeologist's dream. The light filtering in through the opening in the roof told him that. Soon the sun would burn directly into the room. By that time the Staff of Ra would have to be in place to catch the sun's rays as it was designed to do.

Indy got down on his hands and knees and looked closely at the slots in the tile floor. Each slot was marked with a different time of year. When he found the slot he was looking for, Indy set the Staff of Ra into it. Then he waited.

Moment after hushed moment went by. Then the sunlight coming in from above hit the Staff of Ra. Passing through the crystal eye in the headpiece, the golden rays became one intense beam of red light. Indy's eyes followed the beam to where it struck—a building on the outskirts of the model city. Suddenly that building was lit by an unearthly reddish glow.

"The Well of the Souls," Indy murmured. For a brief second, he was awestruck. Then he moved fast. Using a tape measure, a piece of paper and a pencil, he calculated the exact location of the Well of the Souls. With a grin he saw the mark Belloq had made on the model to show the location of the Lost Ark. It was far from the right place. "This time you lose, Belloq," he said. Only then did Indy remember the dangerous spot he was in. He glanced up.

The Map Room lay in a deep hole that the Nazis had dug. Right now Sallah was waiting at the edge of the hole to pull him out. At least Indy hoped Sallah was there. With so many Nazis around, anything could go wrong.

Indy put the headpiece in his pocket. He broke the wooden staff in two and buried it. Then he called Sallah. First softly. Then loudly.

A rope of tied-together rags ending with a Nazi flag came down through the hole in the ceiling. Indy climbed it hand over hand. Soon he was standing with his friend.

"I made it back here just in time," Sallah said. "The Nazis had me running errands."

At that moment a German voice shouted, "You, there, go get me

some water! And be quick about it!"

"See what I mean?" said Sallah. "You'd better get out of here right away. One good look at your face and even a Nazi would be smart enough to know you're no Egyptian. I'll see you back in Cairo this afternoon."

Sallah went off in one direction, Indy in another. Hunching his shoulders together and keeping his face down, Indy headed for the edge of the diggings. Behind a sand dune, he knew, Sallah's truck was waiting.

"Hey, you, come here!" a Nazi shouted. Indy didn't look back to see if the Nazi was shouting at him. He ducked into the nearest tent. He was in luck. It seemed empty. Then, as his eyes adjusted to the dim light, Indy saw a shape struggling in the corner. He moved closer.

"It can't be," he said.

"It is," answered Marion Ravenwood, when he took the gag out of her mouth. "Don't just stand there. Do something."

Indy kissed her. Suddenly it seemed as natural as it had ten years ago, when they were in love.

"I thought you were dead," said Indy. "I thought you were in the truck that exploded."

"That's what he told me," said Marion.

"Who told you?"

"Belloq. It struck him as very funny — you thinking that you had

killed me."

For a moment Indy was so angry he couldn't speak. "Some joke," he finally managed to say.

"He's had me here in his tent since yesterday, Indy. Thank God you've come. Untie me — quick!"

Indy reached for the ropes binding her. Then he stopped. "If they find you missing," Indy said, "they'll double the guard around here. I can't afford that. You see, I've found out where the Ark is. I need just a little more time to get it. I'm afraid you're going to have to stay here for now."

"Why, *you* . . ." Marion began. She stopped and shook her head. "Belloq was right about you."

"What do you mean?"

"He said you're really just the same as he is. That you'll stop at nothing to get what you want. He said I might just as well be his . . . his partner . . . as yours."

Indy hesitated. He wanted to tell her that he'd sacrifice the Lost Ark for her. He wanted to — but he couldn't.

All he could say was, "Look, I can't argue now."

"Well, I can do something," said Marion. "I can start screaming. I can . . ."

"I hate to do this," said Indy, shoving the gag back in her mouth. "I promise I'll be back to get you just as soon as I get the Ark." He kissed her gently on the forehead, right above her angrily blazing eyes.

"So this is the Well of the Souls," said Indy. He and Sallah and their crew had been digging all through the night. Now, just before dawn, they had found what they were looking for.

Thrusting a flaming torch into the darkness, Indy peered down into the chamber. It was thirty feet deep. Its walls were covered with ancient writings. Huge stone statues, like giant guards, stood against the walls. At the far end of the chamber, on an elaborately carved platform, was a thick stone chest. Indy's eyes lit up. He knew that the chest could hold only one thing—the Lost Ark.

Then he noticed something else in the Well of the Souls. "What's that gray stuff all over the floor?" he wondered.

Indy's eyes squinted as he tried to see. Then his face grew pale in the torchlight. Swallowing hard, he dropped a flaming torch into the well. Instantly the air was filled with the sound of angry hissing, and the "gray stuff" began to move. Covering the floor of the well was a deadly carpet of writhing snakes. Asps. The most poisonous snakes in Egypt.

"Why snakes?" said Indy. "Why did it have to be snakes?" He turned to Sallah. "I might as well tell you a little secret about me. There's just one thing in the world I'm really scared of. Guess what it is." Indy looked down at the sea of writhing reptiles. Their eyes were gleaming, their poisonous tongues flicking. "Snakes."

"At least they're not on the platform with the Ark," said Sallah. "They seem to be keeping away from it."

"Nothing is going to keep *me* away from it—not even them," said Indy. Still, for a moment, the sight of the snakes made his stomach turn over. Then he swallowed, and forced himself into action. "We'll need cans of oil from the truck."

Indy and Sallah tossed the cans of oil into the well. Next they lowered down a large wooden crate, using several thick ropes. Arming themselves with flaming torches, they climbed down the ropes after

the crate. As they landed, they used their torches to beat the snakes back. There were thousands of them, Indy saw, piled and entwined six inches deep.

He was covered with cold sweat as he grabbed an oil can and splashed a trail of oil toward the platform of the Ark. He set the oil aflame. As the angry snakes retreated from the fire, Indy and Sallah raced for the platform. Each held a long wooden pole.

"We're safe as long as we're up here," said Indy. The thousands of gleaming reptile eyes stopped six inches or so from the platform. "There's something up here that they're scared of. I'll bet I know what it is. Come on, Sallah, old boy, it's time to see what we've been digging for."

Indy and Sallah took hold of the stone cover of the chest. Their muscles strained as they slowly began to lift it.

"Listen!" said Sallah. "What's that? There's a humming sound coming from inside the chest."

"Keep lifting the cover," said Indy. "We've come too far to turn back now."

At last the heavy stone cover was off. For a moment the light in the well was almost blinding. Uncovered for the first time in centuries, the golden Ark blazed furiously. It was the most beautiful thing Indy had ever seen. With their solemn faces and their shining wings spread wide, the golden angels of the Ark seemed to breathe with life. Indy stared, spellbound. Though the humming of the Ark grew louder and louder, he barely noticed.

Then, from above, came a gigantic thunderclap. It was followed by another, and then another. Soon the night air was booming with thunder, and bolts of lightning were crackling against the dark sky. Indy and Sallah looked at each other in wonder. The humming of the Ark grew louder.

Not far away, Belloq heard the thunder, too. The Frenchman had just come out of his tent to take a breath of air. He had been up all night trying to figure out how his calculations about the Ark had gone wrong. Now it was almost dawn. But with the thunder, the sky had turned dark again. Belloq watched as the lightning flashed again and again above a single spot on the horizon. Strange, he thought. Then his face lit up. There is only one thing that could bring thunder and lightning to this desert, he

thought. The Ark. Somebody has found it for me. And I have a good idea who he is. Belloq shook his head, almost regretfully. I suppose I must now wake up the Nazis, he mused. It's a pity I can't find more civilized helpers. They're really no better than the Hovitos. Belloq hurried off to rouse Dietrich, the Nazi commander.

Inside the Well of the Souls, Indy was in a hurry, too. The flames from the oil were dying. In a few minutes, the snakes would start closing in. Indy did not want to think about what they would do to him if they got close enough.

Then he saw Sallah leaning over to lift the Ark out of the stone chest. Just in time, Indy grabbed his arm.

"Don't touch the Ark, whatever you do," Indy warned. "Remember the warning on the headpiece. We'll use our poles to carry it.

That's what the rings in the Ark are for."

By the time the two men had reached the wooden crate and lowered the Ark into it, the flames had gone out. Indy splashed fresh oil in a circle around them, and lit it.

"You go first," he said to Sallah. "I'll stay down here to make sure the crate gets off the ground."

Sallah went up the rope. Next the crate holding the Ark was slowly lifted to the surface. Finally it was Indy's turn. He took hold of the rope. But when he pulled on it, the rope came tumbling down to land in a heap beside him. Indy looked up, startled.

"Why, Professor Jones, what are you doing in such a nasty place?" asked a familiar voice with a French accent.

Belloq's smiling face looked down at Indy over the rim of the hole. It was joined by the face of Dietrich, Hitler's personal representative. Then came the pudgy face of Toht, the Nazi agent. Beside him was the terrified face of Marion Ravenwood.

"We must go now," Dietrich called to Indy. "But do not think we are heartless. We will not leave you here alone."

Belloq's face registered surprise. "What do you mean . . . ?" he began.

But already Toht had pitched Marion over the side of the hole. Screaming, she fell through the air. Indy dropped his torch and caught her, but the force of her fall smashed him to the ground. Stunned, he found himself staring into the eyes of a snake, an inch from his face. He jerked back just in time to escape its fangs.

"I promised you I'd get you out of Belloq's tent," he said to Marion.

"I knew I could depend on you," she answered.

"Marion, my dear," Belloq called down. "I must apologize for this. I had others plans for you, believe me."

Before Marion could reply, a stone slab closed off the opening. The brightening sky vanished. Now the only light in the well was the flame of Indy's torch and its reflection in thousands of gleaming snakes' eyes.

"You got me into this," said Marion, backing away as far as she could from the hissing snakes. "Now get me out."

"You always used to like excitement," teased Indy.

"I've changed," she said.

"I hope I live to enjoy it," Indy grinned.

"Stop joking," said Marion, staring as if hypnotized at the slithering mass of reptiles coming closer. *"Do something."*

Indy stared up at a huge stone statue towering above them. Silently he handed Marion his torch. He pulled out his bullwhip, and curled its long lash up around the statue's neck. Then he clambered up to the statue's shoulder.

Indy put his whip back in his leather jacket. He wrapped his arms around the statue's neck. "Watch out below!" he shouted as he pushed with his feet against the wall of the well.

The statue swayed. Indy pushed harder. The statue tilted and hung motionless. One more violent push. The statue toppled over like a giant tree falling.

Marion leapt out of its way. There was a tremendous crash, and the statue fell on its side. Its head had smashed a hole through the wall. Indy was nowhere to be seen.

Then Marion heard him calling from the hole. "Follow me in!"

Indy was waiting for her on the other side of the wall. "This is part of a maze of underground rooms," he said. "And no snakes, thank God."

"I'd almost prefer the snakes to *this*," said Marion as they started through the maze. It smelled of rot. Mummies wrapped in decaying cloth lined the walls. Heaps of human skulls were piled high everywhere.

"Look!" said Indy.

In front of them was a sliver of light. Indy started to pull away

the loose bricks around it. Marion joined him. Soon they stood in the sunshine, on a high sand dune.

"Next stop, Cairo," said Marion. "A shower will feel great."

"First we have to do one little thing," said Indy.

"What's that?"

"Get the Ark," he said. "Look down there."

Below them was an airstrip that the Nazis had built. On it was what looked like a giant wing.

"That must be a Flying Wing," said Indy. "It's a new kind of cargo plane. Looks fast. I'll bet the Nazis are planning to carry the Ark back to Hitler in it."

Indy was right. In the Nazi camp, the final preparations for departure were being made. The crate holding the Ark was ringed by armed soldiers. The Nazi officers were packing their bags.

"Before we leave, let's celebrate our triumph," said Belloq.

"Why not?" said Dietrich. "We have time. The plane is still being fueled."

"I am glad the woman has been disposed of," said Toht. "She was very annoying." He looked at the burn scar on his hand. It was his souvenir of the Raven—a perfect copy of the headpiece burned into his flesh.

"I *still* don't know why the copy of the headpiece I made didn't work," said Belloq, giving Toht's burn one last puzzled look. "Your scar was as clear as a photograph!" Then his face brightened. "But what does it matter? We have the Ark. Put *this* in your hand, Toht," he said, and handed the Nazi a champagne glass. He pulled the cork from a champagne bottle. There was a loud pop. At that moment, there was a much louder explosion in the distance. A huge fireball rose in the sky.

A soldier came running up. "The plane, sir," he said. "It exploded!"

"Sabotage!" Toht's voice was enraged.

"We must get the Ark to safety!" said Belloq.

"Put it in the truck," Dietrich ordered the guards. "We'll drive it to Cairo. We can fly it to Germany from there."

"Make sure it has plenty of protection," said Belloq. "We are too close to success to take chances."

Indy and Marion were watching the Nazis from behind a sand dune when Sallah found them. "My friends!" he nearly shouted. "I am so glad to find you alive! But what has happened to you?" he asked. Their faces and clothes were blackened with smoke.

"We tried to swipe a plane," said Indy. "But we couldn't. So we had to get rid of it."

"We almost got rid of ourselves, too," said Marion. "And speaking of getting rid of things, what are we going to do about *that*?" She pointed to the desert below, where Dietrich and his men were loading the crated Ark into the back of a truck. Nine armed soldiers climbed into the truck and stationed themselves around the Ark. Sitting behind the truck was an open staff car, mounted with a large black machine gun.

"I don't know," said Indy. "But I'll think of something." He turned to Sallah. "Take care of her," he said. "I'll see you later, in Cairo." Keeping low, he darted off.

Marion and Sallah were left to watch as Dietrich, Belloq, and an armed guard climbed into an open car in front of the truck. Toht, a driver, and a gunner got

into the car in back of the truck. Dietrich shouted a command, and the convoy moved off in a cloud of dust.

Suddenly a new cloud of dust appeared. A fiery white Arabian stallion came galloping across the desert after the Nazis. Its rider was Indy.

Marion smiled in wonder, as Indy and the horse disappeared after the convoy. "I guess he *will* do anything to get the Ark," she said.

The Nazi soldier sitting beside the driver of the truck was struck by wonder, too. He looked out his side window and found himself staring into the eyes of a smoke-blackened man in a leather jacket and battered felt hat, riding a great white stallion. Then the truck door was yanked open. The soldier was pulled out of his seat

and tossed out of the truck. Indy jumped in through the wildly swinging door. He started fighting the driver for the steering wheel.

In the car behind, Toht was wild with rage. "You fool!" he screamed at his machine gunner. "How could you miss a man on a horse! Such a beautiful target!"

"The bumps on this road," said the gunner. "And the curves. And the dust. It is impossible to shoot straight."

As if to prove his point, the car swerved into a narrow hairpin turn. The dirt road was running through desert mountains now. It twisted and turned, rose and dipped, like a roller coaster designed by a maniac.

Toht's face turned red and he began to swear. "Faster! Faster!" he yelled at his driver.

"But this road . . ." the driver protested.

"Faster!" Toht shouted.

The driver had to obey. He raced the car into the cloud of dust left by the truck—and right over the edge of a curve into empty space. "Idiot!" screamed Toht, as he realized, too late, where they were going. A moment later the car was a flaming heap at the bottom of a deep ravine.

Dietrich and Belloq, leading the convoy, could not see what had happened to Toht's car. But they could see Indy and the truck driver struggling behind them. Part of the time Indy and the driver fought each other for control of the steering wheel. Part of the time they had to join together to keep the truck from crashing out of control.

"Kill the American swine! Get rid of him for good!" Dietrich ordered his machine gunner. The gunner nodded. Smiling, he aimed his weapon.

"Don't touch the trigger!" Belloq commanded.

"Do not interfere with the orders of a Nazi officer!" said Dietrich. His hand went to his holster.

"Hitler does not want an American corpse," said Belloq. "He wants the Ark. If the truck crashes and the Ark is destroyed, due to your orders . . ."

Dietrich realized that Belloq was right. "Hold your fire!" he shouted to the gunner.

"Anyway, your soldiers will soon have the situation under control," said Belloq. "Look." Nazi soldiers were climbing out of the back of the truck and edging along its sides. The first ones had almost reached the driver's compartment when the car and then the truck sped into a narrow tunnel.

When the truck came out of the tunnel, its sides had been swept clean by the tunnel walls. "That American has the luck of the devil," Dietrich snarled.

"You can say good-bye to the driver, too," said Belloq, as the driver was sent flying out the door. Indy had taken complete control of the truck.

"We still have one more good soldier," said Dietrich. "He is one of our best men. He will do the job."

A Nazi sergeant was creeping over the top of the driver's compartment. He leaned over the side to look down through the window at Indy. Indy didn't see him. His eyes were fixed on the road. The Nazi's pistol was pointed straight at Indy's head.

"Your brilliant soldier is going to shoot," groaned Belloq. "Say good-bye to the truck and the Ark."

A shot rang out. The pistol dropped out of the sergeant's hand. The sergeant's body dropped off the truck. Dietrich put his pistol back in his holster.

"That is the price that must be paid for mistakes," said Dietrich. His face was grim. "We cannot let that truck escape!"

"Don't worry," said Belloq. "It can't get by us. All we have to do is . . ." Belloq stopped in mid-sentence. The truck was gaining on them every second. Indy had jumped up the speed. "Dietrich!" shouted Belloq. "Tell your driver to . . ."

Belloq's warning came too late. The truck smashed into the back of the Nazi car. There was a sickening crunch, and the car went flying off the road. By the time it had come to a stop, the truck was almost out of sight.

"Hurry up! Follow it!" Dietrich shouted to the driver. The car engine roared. The wheels spun, and spun again. The car did not move. It was stuck in the sand.

Belloq leaped out of the car. He looked down the road. Far off in the distance, a tiny cloud of dust was speeding toward the hazy outline of Cairo. "I'll get you yet, Indiana Jones," Belloq vowed softly. "I have always beaten you. And I always will."

"It's clear sailing from here on in," said Marion to Indy. "They'll never find us now."

She stood beside him at the rail of a ship that was heading out into the Mediterranean. Though it was old, rusty, and battered, the *Bantu Wind* moved along at a steady clip. It was used to hurrying. Its trade was piracy.

"It's lucky for us that Sallah knew the captain," said Indy. "Katanga may be a pirate, but I'd trust him with my life."

"You flatter me," said a voice behind them. It was Katanga. His black skin gleamed in the sun. His muscles rippled beneath his open shirt. His white teeth flashed as he smiled. "I hope you are enjoying your trip. Please tell me if any of my crew bothers you. Sometimes their manners can be a trifle rough."

"Compared to the Nazis, they're absolute angels," said Marion.

"We really appreciate the favor you're doing us," said Indy. "As soon as you deliver us and our cargo to a safe port, I'll make sure you're rewarded."

"Speaking of your . . . cargo," said Katanga, "the humming coming from it continues to grow louder. It has started to scare away even the rats in the ship's hold." He looked at Indy closely. "I trust it is not dangerous."

"Just make sure none of your crew opens it," said Indy.

"Don't worry about that," said Katanga. "I've seen some of my men charge into the mouths of cannon. But none of them wants to go near that wooden crate."

Suddenly a loud voice blaring through a bullhorn cut off their conversation.

"Stop your ship immediately. Prepare to be boarded."

A Nazi submarine had broken through the surface of the sea. Its deck guns were trained on the *Bantu Wind*. Already rafts packed with armed Nazi sailors were moving toward the pirate ship.

"Do not think of resisting!" the Nazi voice boomed out. *"We can blow you out of the water in a minute!"*

"He's right, Katanga," Indy said. "Don't try to fight. Getting you and your crew killed wasn't part of our deal."

"You must hide," said Katanga. "Quick." The pirate captain saw Indy and Marion heading below decks together. "Separate," he said. "You will be harder to find."

There was no time to discuss the matter. The Nazi rafts had reached the ship. Indy made sure that

Marion was safely on the ladder going below. Then he desperately searched for a hiding place of his own.

He saw a ventilator opening in the shadow of the ship's bridge. He could just fit through it. Feeling like a human pretzel, he squeezed himself into the curved ventilator shaft. From its darkness he could watch the action on deck.

Indy's hands clenched into fists when he saw the first boarder to come over the rail. It was Belloq. Next came Dietrich. They were followed by a crowd of armed Nazis.

"Search everywhere for the Americans and the Ark," Dietrich shouted. "We know they are here."

"They most certainly should be," said Belloq, "considering the money we paid for the information on the Cairo waterfront."

A moment later, Marion was dragged kicking and screaming up from below deck.

"If you had asked me," Katanga said, "I would have told you where she was. Just like I will tell you where Indy Jones is."

In the ventilator shaft, Indy tensed.

"Where is he?" Belloq asked eagerly.

"Dead. At the bottom of the sea," said Katanga. "What use was he to me? She is more valuable. I was going to sell her at the

slave market. I hope you will pay me for her."

"You are lucky we don't want to waste good ammunition on you," said Dietrich. "Scum like you doesn't deserve to live."

"I still can't believe that Jones would let himself . . ." Belloq began. Then he saw the crate with the Lost Ark being hauled onto the deck. "We have it!" he said, his voice rising with excitement. "We must load it onto the submarine and be off! I have waited too long for this already."

"Yes," said Dietrich. "Hitler must be getting impatient." Katanga stood at the rail glumly as the Nazis returned to their submarine. "And they call me a pirate," he muttered.

"They took Marion?" asked Indy. He had left his hiding place to join Katanga.

"Yes," Katanga answered. "And the Ark, too, unfortunately."

"It might not submerge," Indy said, thinking out loud. "They can travel much faster if they stay on the surface."

"What are you talking about?" asked Katanga. "What are you doing? Are you crazy?"

But Indy was already over the rail, swimming for the submarine. He hoisted himself onto its deck and moved toward its conning tower. Then he felt a trembling beneath him. The submarine was going under! Sea water sloshed around Indy's feet. He raced to the conning tower and started up the ladder to the top. The water followed him. At the top of the tower, he grabbed the periscope and hauled himself higher. Inch by inch the water crept up above his waist. When it reached his neck, Indy took a deep breath. He knew it might be his last.

Then the sub stopped going down. It began to speed forward instead. Indy breathed a long sigh of relief. The Nazis were in too much of a hurry to submerge. For the moment, his life was safe.

Pulling his bullwhip out from under his jacket, Indy used it to tie himself to the periscope. As the sun set, he closed his eyes and fell into a deep, exhausted sleep.

"This sure doesn't look like Germany," was his first thought on waking. The sub was heading straight for a tiny, semitropical island with a tall mountain at its center. As the submarine approached, Indy could see the mouth of what looked like a huge cave. When they were closer still, he saw that the cave was actually a large submarine pen. The island was a secret Nazi base! But why

had they come here, while Hitler was waiting impatiently for the Ark in Berlin?

Inside the submarine, Dietrich was wondering the same thing. "I still say this is all French foolishness," the Nazi said to Belloq. "We should go directly to the Fatherland. Our greatest scientists are there, ready to put the Ark to work."

"None of them knows as much about the Ark as I do," said Belloq. "For years I have been preparing for the day when it would be in my hands."

"What do you mean, *your* hands?" asked Dietrich.

"I am at your service, of course," said Belloq quickly. "My skill and my knowledge are at your disposal. But it would be a terrible mistake to bring the Ark to Hitler without opening it first. How else will you know if you have truly accomplished your mission?"

"I suppose you have a point," said Dietrich. "But all this mumbo-jumbo that you insist on—it is not the Nazi way. We would simply open up the Ark and look inside."

"I am following the rules laid down by the ancients," said Belloq. "They alone knew how to unleash the power inside the Ark. You don't want to risk damaging it, do you?"

"Absolutely not," said Dietrich. "Nazi Germany must have its power, and soon." He smiled at the thought. "If this works, Belloq, I will personally see that you get a bonus."

"I'll take the woman," said Belloq. "It will be amusing to break down her resistance."

"Sometimes I think you might have the makings of a good Nazi," Dietrich told him.

"You flatter me," said Belloq. He could barely conceal his sarcasm.

Then a voice came crackling over the loudspeaker. "Attention! We are surfacing."

"At last," cried Belloq. He leaped to his feet. "Unload the Ark immediately! There is still time to perform the ceremony today!"

Standing on the island, Belloq looked around with satisfaction. It was the perfect place for the ritual he was about to perform. High on the mountainside above was a

great, flat outcropping of rock. Shadowed by a huge stone idol, it formed a natural altar. The wide steps carved into the mountainside must have been used by priests long ago, thought Belloq as he got ready.

Carefully he donned the multicolored silk robes of an Israelite high priest. Then, climbing the steps, he began to chant. His voice, singing in Hebrew, grew louder as he climbed closer to the altar. There, humming steadily, the glowing gold Ark of the Covenant awaited him.

Below him, the Nazis looked and listened, muttering among themselves. In their front rank, Dietrich's face grew dark with outrage as he realized that Belloq's prayers were in Hebrew. Standing between two Nazi guards, Marion Ravenwood could not tear her eyes away from the strange spectacle.

"Hold it right there!" came a voice from behind a grenade launcher. Though the weapon and the uniform were German, the voice was definitely American.

"One more move from anybody, and I blow the Ark back to Moses!"

"Jones!" exclaimed Belloq. "I should have known you weren't dead."

"How dare you wear the uniform of a Nazi soldier!" screamed Dietrich. "Do you think it will do you any good? You will never escape from this island! It is a Nazi fortress!"

"Calm down," said Indy. "All I want is Marion. We'll keep the Ark only until we're sure of safe passage to England. Then you can have it back."

"And if I refuse?" said Dietrich.

"Then the Ark is going to go up with a big bang," said Indy. "I don't think Hitler would like that one bit."

"Let us not argue," said Belloq. "Of course we agree. Though I must say I'm disappointed in you, Jones. Choosing the woman over the Ark. I never would have believed it." Then Belloq shouted, "Get him!"

Rough hands grabbed Indy from behind. His grenade launcher was jerked away by the Nazi sol-

diers who had crept up on him.

"Now you will learn what Nazi justice is," said Dietrich, raising his pistol.

"No!" said Belloq. "I insist on my own justice first."

"What do you mean?" asked Dietrich. He clearly did not want to put down his gun.

"Indy Jones is the only archaeologist on earth worthy to be my rival," said Belloq. "He alone has a hunger for the wisdom of the ancients that equals mine. I want him to watch me when I look into the Ark. I want him to know that I am seeing what he will never see. My greatest triumph will be his greatest defeat! Tie him up so he can watch me. After that, do what you want with him. Do you agree?"

"Only if I can have the woman, too," said Dietrich. "She must be destroyed."

Belloq shrugged his shoulders. "I am truly sorry," he said to Marion. "But to achieve one's goals, one must sometimes strike an unpleasant bargain."

"Forget the pretty apology," said Marion, glaring at him.

"Let us get on with it," said Dietrich. "The sun is setting. Soon it will be too dark to see unless we move fast."

"We must do everything correctly," said Belloq. He spoke with an intensity that made even Dietrich back off. "Without haste! Without mistakes! Turn on the lights. Then we will continue."

Soon the lights that had been set up over the altar were shining brightly. Once again Belloq began to chant. As the sound of his voice grew louder, his expression slowly changed. What had once been a smile of triumph became a look of insane, demonic joy.

Tied to the post, Indy and Marion turned to look at each other.

"Indy, I'm so afraid," Marion said.

"There's never been a better time for it," Indy admitted.

"I want you to know something," Marion said.

"I want you to know something, too," said Indy.

"I love you," they said together, just as Belloq's chanting stopped.

Now all that could be heard in the night was the humming of the Ark. It grew louder and louder, as if it would drown out all the other sounds in the world. Indy and Marion turned their heads from side to side in an effort to escape it. Even the Nazis seemed shaken. A few soldiers backed away from the altar holding their ears. Only Belloq, overcome with excitement, did not seem to be affected by it.

Suddenly Indy remembered the warning engraved on the headpiece. "Marion!" he called, hoping his voice would reach her over the humming. "Listen to me! When he opens the Ark, close your eyes. *Don't look!*"

Lifting an ivory rod, Belloq slowly inserted it into the lid of the Ark. The instant the rod touched the Ark, the electric lights exploded. A glittering shower of glass fragments rained down on the altar. But Belloq did not stop. The glow of the Ark had mesmerized him.

"Now I will have the power of God Himself!" he shouted, as he lifted the lid.

Dietrich and his men moved closer to share Belloq's view.

"Don't look, Marion!" shouted Indy at the top of his lungs as the Ark's humming grew even louder. "Shut your eyes tight!"

Indy breathed a sigh of relief when he saw Marion close her eyes. Then he shut his eyes too.

Indy could not see the Ark as it unleashed the full force of its almighty power. He could not see its dazzling light, stronger than a thousand suns, shooting up into the heavens.

He could not see Belloq's face, or the faces of the Nazis, when that light met their astonished eyes.

He could not see those eyes grow blind, or those faces burning, dissolving, and dying away as the Ark's unearthly light consumed them.

All that Indy knew, after the roaring and the light had ended and the lid of the Ark had slammed shut, was that he was free. The ropes tying him to the post had turned to ash.

"Can I look now?" Marion's whisper was frightened.

For a moment Indy was speechless at the sight that met his eyes. Then he said, "Yes. But brace yourself."

Marion looked. "What on earth happened?" she gasped.

She and Indy were completely alone. All that remained of Belloq and the Nazis was a pile of ashes, drifting slowly now on the ground near the altar.

"They looked inside the Ark," said Indy.

The Ark was glowing brightly in the darkness of the island night. Its angels, with their shimmering wings spread wide, seemed to vibrate with life. And though the Ark's hum was quiet now, it went on steadily, as if it would never stop.

"I know this sounds terrible," said Marion, "but they deserved what they got. They never should have opened it. Belloq, at least, should have known better."

"He refused to believe in its power," said Indy. "He thought he could use it—the way he used everything else. And he was wrong. The Ark isn't just another relic. It's something much, much greater." He gazed at it with fascination. "A power beyond human control."

"The sooner it's out of your hands, the better," Marion said firmly. "The U.S. Government will be happy to have it."

"I only hope they'll know what to do with it," said Indy, with a doubtful shake of his head.

"Of course we'll give the matter our most careful attention," the high American official promised Indy. "Now, please accept this check as payment for your services."

There was a polite murmur as Indy took the money. With him in the Washington office were Marion, Marcus Brody, Colonel Musgrove, and Major Eaton.

Indy barely looked at the check in his hand. "There's a lot of research that should be done on the Ark—and right away," he said.

"Of course, of course," said Colonel Musgrove.

"Brody and I could be of great help," Indy said.

"We'll certainly keep you in mind," said Major Eaton.

"You have to realize how important the Ark is," Indy insisted.

"It's not the only thing in the world that's important," said Marion. She put her arms around Indy's neck and kissed him.

"Why don't you two go out and start spending some of that money," said the government official with an encouraging smile.

"Don't worry about the Ark, Professor Jones. We know how to handle it."

When Indy and Marion had left with the others, the official picked up his phone and dialed a number. "That crate I had delivered to your warehouse," he said. "Did it arrive safely?"

"Yes, sir," said the voice on the other end. "What should we do with it?"

"What do you think?" asked the official impatiently. "Store it away, of course. It will have to wait its turn to be examined."

Again the Ark was in a wooden crate. This time the crate was clearly marked: "TOP SECRET. ARMY INTELLIGENCE #9906753. DO NOT OPEN!"

An elderly man rolled a cart with the crate on it down a long aisle in a dusty warehouse. On each side of the aisle were stacks of crates, all the same size. The entire warehouse was filled with crates, thousands and thousands of them, all marked "TOP SECRET!"

The man set the crate down among the others. Then he went away. Before long the first specks of dust were settling on it. Soon it would seem like all the others. Except for one thing: the low humming. The humming that warned man not to lift its lid. The humming that seemed to say that the Ark knew that now it never would be lost again.

Outside, the world continued to move toward a war that would make both sides search desperately for the key to victory. And inside the Ark, the humming went on and on.